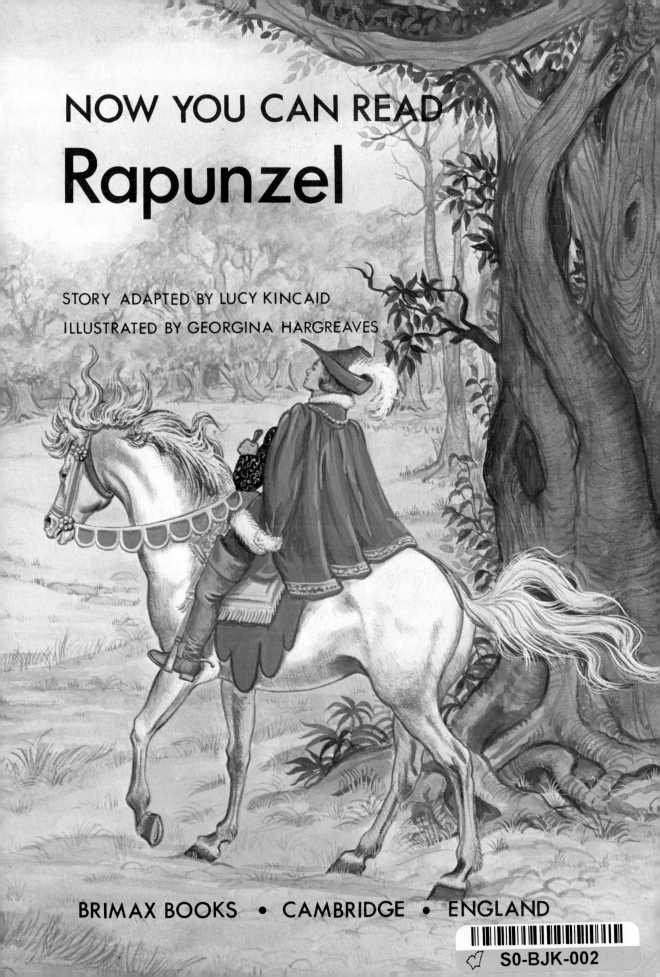

NOW YOU CAN READ
Rapunzel

STORY ADAPTED BY LUCY KINCAID

ILLUSTRATED BY GEORGINA HARGREAVES

BRIMAX BOOKS • CAMBRIDGE • ENGLAND

A Prince was riding his horse in the forest. He could hear someone singing. The voice was beautiful but the song was very sad. Where was the voice coming from? The Prince could not see anyone.

The Prince rode on. When he
came to the middle of the forest,
he could see a very tall tower.
The voice was coming from a small
window at the top. The Prince
walked round and round the tower
looking for a way in. There was
no way in. The tower had no door.

The Prince went back to the forest the next day. He climbed a tree near the tower. He sat and listened to the voice which sang so sweetly and yet so sadly.

"If only I could see into the tower," said the Prince.

"If only I could see who the voice belongs to."

Presently an old witch came out of the forest. The Prince stayed hidden and watched her.

She went to the foot of the tower. "Rapunzel!" she called. "Let down your hair!"

A long braid of golden hair came tumbling from the window at the top of the tower. It was so long it reached the ground.

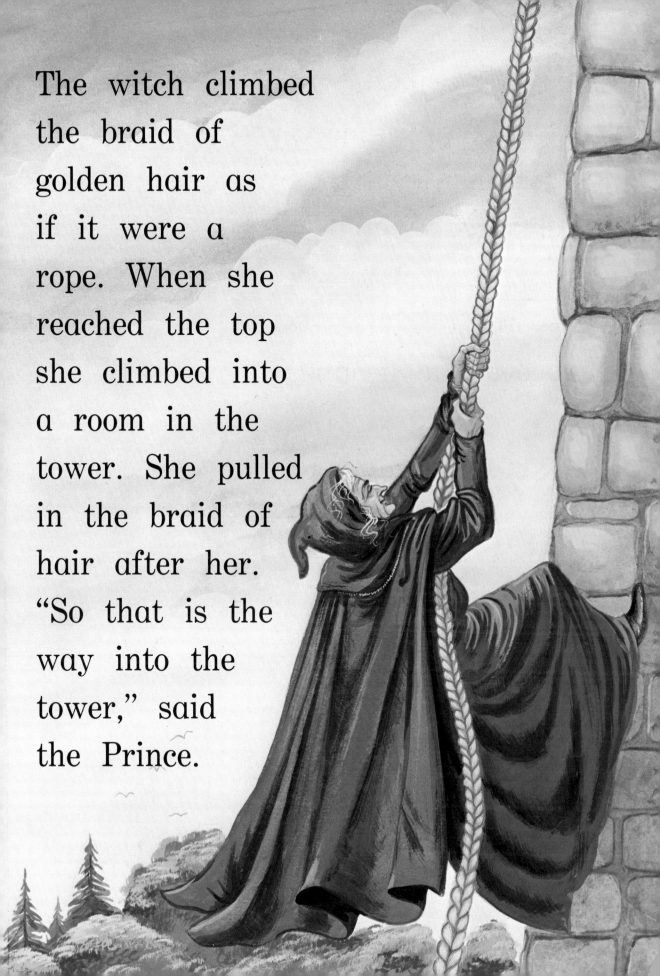

The witch climbed the braid of golden hair as if it were a rope. When she reached the top she climbed into a room in the tower. She pulled in the braid of hair after her. "So that is the way into the tower," said the Prince.

Presently the braid
of hair fell from
the window again.
The witch climbed
down by it and went
off into the forest.
Someone inside the
tower pulled the
hair back again.

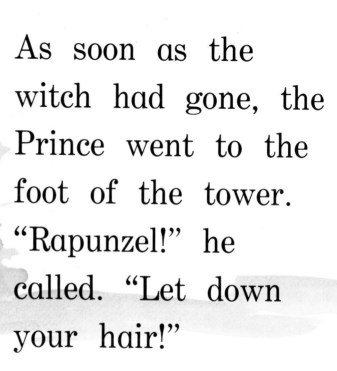

As soon as the
witch had gone, the
Prince went to the
foot of the tower.
"Rapunzel!" he
called. "Let down
your hair!"

The braid of hair came tumbling down, just as it had when the witch called. But this time it was the Prince who climbed it like a rope. "I wonder who I will find at the top?" said the Prince to himself.

At the top of the tower was a tiny room. In the room was a beautiful girl. The long golden hair was hers. The witch had kept her in the tower since she was a small girl. She was a prisoner. That is why she sang so sadly.

"Tomorrow I will bring a ladder made from silk and help you to escape," said the Prince.

The old witch found out that Rapunzel had seen the Prince. She was very angry. She was very angry indeed. She wanted to keep Rapunzel hidden away from everyone. "You will never see the Prince again!" she cried as she took a pair of scissors from the table.

She cut right
through the braid
of golden hair.
It fell to the
floor and lay in
a shining heap.
"Now let the Prince try to climb
into the tower," cried the witch.
Then because she was so angry,
she banished Rapunzel to a far-away
land.

Next day the Prince returned to the tower. "Rapunzel!" he called. "Let down your hair!" The long braid of golden hair came tumbling to the ground. The Prince thought Rapunzel had let it down.

The Prince began the long climb upwards. He had a silken ladder tucked inside his coat. Rapunzel would soon be free.

He had almost reached the window when he looked up, and saw the witch looking down at him. She was holding the braid of golden hair in her hands.

"You will never see Rapunzel again!" said the wicked witch. She opened her fingers and let the braid of golden hair slip through them. It fell to the stony ground far, far below. The poor Prince fell to the stony ground with it.

The Prince lay on the ground for a long time. When, at last, he opened his eyes he could not see. He was blind.

He wandered far and wide, thinking only of Rapunzel. He was very sad for he could not think of a way to help her.

Then one day, when he was far
from home, he heard someone singing
The song was both sweet and sad.
It was a song he had heard before.
He could not see, but the Prince
knew he had found Rapunzel.

Rapunzel kissed his blind eyes and he could see again.

The Prince took Rapunzel home to his castle and they lived happily ever after. The spell of the wicked witch was broken and she was never seen again.

tower

tree

horse

Prince

All these appear in the pages of the story. Can you find them?